The Dr. Cage Chronicles:
Memoirs of a Sex Therapist

I Think I'm a Serial Swiper

THE DR. CAGE CHRONICLES:
MEMOIRS OF A SEX THERAPIST

I Think I'm a Serial Swiper

GRAYSON ACE

4 Horsemen
Publications, Inc.

I Think I'm a Serial Swiper
Copyright © 2020 Grayson Ace. All rights reserved.

4 Horsemen Publications, Inc.

4 Horsemen Publications, Inc.
1497 Main St. Suite 169
Dunedin, FL 34698
4horsemenpublications.com
info@4horsemenpublications.com

Cover & Typesetting by Battle Goddess Productions
Editor Nita Edetor

All rights to the work within are reserved to the author and publisher. No part of this publication may be reproduced, stored in a retrieval system, or transmitted in any form or by any means, electronic, mechanical, photocopying, recording, scanning, or otherwise, except as permitted under Section 107 or 108 of the 1976 International Copyright Act, without prior written permission except in brief quotations embodied in critical articles and reviews. Please contact either the Publisher or Author to gain permission.

This is a work of fiction. All characters, organizations, and events portrayed in this novel are either products of the author's imagination or are used fictitiously.

E-Book ISBN: ISBN: 978-1-64450-152-8
Print ISBN: ISBN: 978-1-64450-154-2

This book is dedicated to the haters who can't seem to keep my name out of their mouth.

Chapter 1

ROCKY'S SWIPING

After my session with Rocky and the two bottoms, I knew that there was no way that Rocky would be going back to Pennsylvania. When we got home that night, he asked if he could stay permanently. Naturally, I agreed, because I loved having him in San Francisco with me.

Rocky decided to go back to school to study psychology. After seeing how good I am at my job, he said that he wanted to follow in my footsteps. It definitely made me feel good that

I Think I'm a Serial Swiper

my older brother looked up to me. Although my treatments might be a bit unorthodox, I must have been doing something right. I swear, though, that between my phone and his, the only sound I heard in the house was the sound of dating apps going off.

Rocky spent a lot of time on dating apps, which I totally understood. When I was new in the gay scene, all I wanted to do was meet guys and hook up. He'd only been with a few guys, so I knew he was going to want to get it out of his system. One night after dinner, as Rocky was looking down at his phone, I noticed his hand continually going in one direction. I asked him what he was doing, and he said, "I'm swiping right." I already knew that but wanted to know why he was swiping right on so many guys instead of swiping left.

"I just wanna fuck," he responded. I also already knew that and told him he needed to play it safe and be careful. He rolled his eyes, called me "Dad," and continued swiping. I knew what it was like to be in his shoes, so I needed to let him experience these things on his own.

Chapter 2

SNEAKY LITTLE FUCK

The following morning, I heard Rocky rustling around in the kitchen. The sun hadn't even come up yet, and when I looked at the alarm, it was only 5am. I got up to see what he was doing just in time to see him grab something out of the basket by the front door and bolt toward the door. I yelled his name, and he stopped, turned around, and said he was going to the gym. Rocky never went to the gym, so I knew something was up.

After Rocky left, I looked in the basket to see what he had grabbed. Noticing the keys to my office were missing, I quickly threw on some clothes and headed to my office. I knew what he was about to do and can't say I wouldn't have done the same thing in his situation.

I got to the office, and naturally the little asshole didn't even bother locking the door behind him. Slowly, I opened the door, and I could already hear a man moaning. Closing the door gently, I made sure they couldn't hear me in the office. The guy had a pretty deep voice, which made me wonder if Rocky were going after a Daddy and that's why he didn't want to bring him back to the house.

Tiptoeing through the office until I got to one of the therapy rooms, I noticed that the door was slightly cracked open, the moaning from inside deep and loud. I pushed the door open just enough so I could see what was going on without them noticing me.

I Think I'm a Serial Swiper

Rocky was sprawled out on the couch—arms on the back, legs spread, totally naked, with a sexy naked man kneeling in front of him, bobbing his head up and down on his cock. I didn't realize his voice was so deep when he moaned. The guy on his knees had his back arched while he was blowing my brother, and I could see his hole—perfect as can be and kind of familiar looking. Although, almost every ass I've had has looked the same.

I watched as this guy blew my brother and made him moan in pure pleasure. I could feel my own cock growing and started rubbing it on the outside of my shorts. I wanted to bust in the room and just shove my cock right in this guy's ass as he blew my brother, but that would have been weird. Or would it have been?

I pulled my shorts down just below my balls so I could start stroking my piece. I'm not sure how they didn't know I was there, or maybe they did, and they liked having an audience. When the guy got up from his knees,

I thought he was about to shove his cock inside of Rocky, but he grabbed the lube and started rubbing it on his own hole, crawling up on top of Rocky and devouring his cock with his hole.

Rocky grabbed onto the guy's hips as he lowered himself and immediately started pounding away at this dude's ass. He was like a machine, thrusting his dick in and out of his hole so fast and so hard—I could practically feel it. I started stroking on my own cock even harder, imagining it was me pounding away at this guy's hole.

Rocky pushed the guy up off his dick, turned, and threw him face down on the couch. He got up behind him, pushed his face into the cushion, and shoved his dick deep in his hole. I never thought my brother would be so aggressive, but I must say I was proud of him. As he pounded away at this guy's ass, he held his head down with his hand. The man was letting out some pretty loud screams, and Rocky was getting pretty verbal with him, calling him his little bitch and telling him his hole needed to take it.

Unable to take my eyes off the scene before me, I kept stroking my cock faster and faster. I could feel myself edging towards a climax, but I wanted to hold on as long as possible so I could keep watching. Feeling the rush, I started to shoot my load all over the door. Rocky made one final thrust into this dude's ass, and I knew that he was flooding his hole. The guy pushed his ass back a little bit so he could reach his own cock, and within seconds, he was shooting his batter all over the couch.

I grabbed a towel so I could wipe my jizz off the door, and as I was walking away, the floor made a loud creaking sound. I couldn't let them know that I had just watched, never mind that I had just beat off watching them fuck, so I ran to my desk, put on my headphones, and pretended to be listening to music.

As Rocky came down the hallway and saw me sitting there, he immediately looked like a deer caught in the headlights. I took off my headphones, acting like I hadn't heard anything, and asked what he was doing in the office. He stumbled on his words a bit: "I ran into one of your patients at the gym, and he mentioned he had left something in the office during his session and wanted to get it, so I figured I'd bring him to check it out." I smiled and put my headphones back on. I was about to look back at my computer, but the guy surprised me coming out of the room. It was Ryan, the bottom who was dating John, whom I saw fuck my brother during his last session. Apparently, he was still a bottom.

Chapter 3

WHEN ALL ELSE FAILS—SWIPE

As badly as I wanted to let Rocky know that I had witnessed what happened between him and Ryan, there was no way. I definitely didn't approve of him fucking around with someone who was in a relationship—unless they decided an open relationship worked for them, as most all-bottom couples do.

I knew after basically being caught that Rocky wouldn't be sneaking off to my office anymore for dick appointments. Instead, he got brave and just started bringing guys home, practically every night, thinking I wouldn't hear them. Every morning we'd do the same routine—wake up, say good morning, and smile at each other, knowing what had happened the night before.

I decided I needed to have some fun of my own, and at this point, I didn't even realize how long it had been since the last time I fucked. I grabbed my phone and decided to give the swiping surge a try and see what happened. It seemed to be working for Rocky, although at the rate he had been going, I was likely to swipe on someone that he had already fucked. A little friendly competition couldn't hurt.

I literally started swiping right on every profile—fat, skinny, hot, ugly—it didn't matter. I was swiping right. Messages flooded me almost immediately, and I deleted most of them because they just weren't cute. Maybe I shouldn't have been swiping right, but more

I Think I'm a Serial Swiper

rights meant more choices, and I'd be as picky or lenient as I wanted. After all, an ugly face doesn't necessarily mean a bad fuck.

After going through every profile within a 25 miles radius and swiping right on every last one, I told myself I'd wait at least a day before I started reading and responding to messages. Naturally, I only lasted about an hour, thinking with the head of my dick instead of the one on my shoulders. I was horny and needed some action—now.

No joke—I had messages from 43 different guys. Just glancing at the pictures on the messages, and the few who said "Hey Daddy" as their opening line, I deleted more than half. I went through the remaining messages, responding to some, and leaving others on "read." One specific guy caught my eye–Sean. Sean had a great smile, nice hair, and according to his profile, was six feet tall with an eight-inch cock. I was digging him.

We made small talk for a little bit. You know, the typical "Hey handsome. How's your Friday? Any plans for the weekend?" type of shit. After about twenty minutes of the lame conversation, I finally asked for a dick pic. He must have been waiting for it because I swear this bitch sent it before I could even finish the question. And it was just as he described it in his profile—a beautiful eight inches of perfectly non-curved penis. I was pretty surprised because most of the men I had been with had at least a tiny bit of a curve going with their dicks, but not this guy.

I knew Rocky would be going out, so I asked Sean if he wanted to come over and have a few drinks, and by "a few drinks," I obviously meant "fill me with your load." When he got to my place, he was just as cute as in his pictures, and he gave me a kiss on the cheek as he walked through the door. I didn't even bother pouring drinks, blatantly asking if he wanted to go to

I Think I'm a Serial Swiper

the bedroom. I swear he said yes faster than I could even blink.

I hopped on the bed and pulled him over to me. He leaned down and started kissing me, and I quickly grabbed his shirt and yanked it off. He wasn't ripped or anything but had a decent body with a little bit of a belly, which I always find super sexy. He quickly got right on top of me, making out with his chest on top of mine, slightly grinding his dick on my leg. My hands were all over him, rubbing up and down his back and moving down toward his ass and into his shorts. He had a beautiful ass that felt so good in my hands.

He would move from kissing my mouth to sucking on my neck, pushing my shirt up to suck on my nipples then back up again. I could feel his cock getting hard as he rubbed it against my growing member. I reached down in between our bodies as we were grinding and started rubbing my hand on his dick. Even through his pants, I could tell how big it was.

He started kissing down my neck and onto my chest, making his way down toward my happy trail with his mouth. He pulled my shorts and briefs down and devoured my whole piece with his mouth, not even grabbing onto it with his hands. I could feel my cock pressing against the back of his throat, but this guy didn't even let out a single gag—he was obviously a professional. He kept sucking up and down my shaft, and at one point pulled his own shorts down, releasing that beautiful monster.

He rolled over a bit on his side, never letting my dick escape from his mouth so he could start jerking on his own. I watched in awe as he rubbed his tool, knowing I needed to get a taste of it. I grabbed his head, picked it up off of my cock, and pulled him up toward me. We made out for a few seconds, and then I pulled him up even more to get his dick positioned right in front of my face. I pulled him closer, forcing his warm cock deep into my throat. I grabbed onto his ass cheeks and held them as he fucked my face, slowly at first and then faster as time went on. I reached down and started stroking my dick, letting his ram against the back of my throat without even caring.

After a few minutes, I pushed him off of me and onto his back, telling him I wanted to feel him inside of me. I lubed up his cock, threw one leg over him and slowly lowered my ass down onto his pipe. I wasn't sure if I'd be able to take the entire thing, but it went into my hole with such ease–I didn't even need to give it a minute to stretch before I started bouncing up and down on his perfect cock. He leaned up from the pillow and started kissing me, and he pulled off my shirt. I really don't like having any clothes on during sex, except the occasional sock.

I could feel his cock going deep into my ass and knew I wanted to take his load. I could tell from the look on his face that he wasn't used to the feeling of such a tight ass and wasn't going to last long. He grabbed onto my cock, started stroking it, and said he was getting close. I leaned down to start kissing him, and the moment our tongues touched, I felt him thrust upward and let out a screech, filling my hole.

Sean quickly pushed me off his dick and onto my back, lifted my legs up, and shoved his tongue into my hole. Never in my life had a guy done that to me after filling me with his load, but it was like being in heaven. He told me to push it out, and I could feel it dripping out of my hole. He licked it all back up. I swear he must have emptied me out.

I was still rock hard and hadn't cum yet, so Sean grabbed the lube and poured it all over my dick. I was still on my back, and he basically jumped on top of me and let my cock slide right into his hole. After him eating his cum out of my ass, I knew I wasn't going to last very long. He kept stroking his cock as he was riding mine, and I let out a loud gasp and shot my load right into his hole. He kept thrusting up and down, completely draining my vein deep into his ass.

I Think I'm a Serial Swiper

There was no way I was going to eat my load out of his ass, as tempting as it may be.

Sean spent the night, the first guy I spent the night with in quite a while. The next morning when he was putting his clothes back on, he told me that he had something to tell me. This is one of the worst things someone can say after a night of amazing sex.

"I have herpes."

Really? He couldn't have told me this before I decided to let him blow his load in my hole? I was livid but didn't want to make a scene. I said, "Oh," and that was about it. He left. I immediately went to the clinic to get tested, and thank God, he didn't spread anything to me. Needless to say, I wouldn't be swiping right that much anymore.

Chapter 4

THE LIST

Keeping my word, I hesitated to swipe right on random guys anymore. I had a busy week ahead of me with work, and although getting dick was nice, I knew I needed to switch my focus. Besides, Rocky's bedroom was basically a Texas whorehouse, so I knew I could always grab some sloppy seconds as his marks did their walk of shame out the front door.

I had started to get a lot of repeat patients, so I was pretty excited to have a new one coming in on Monday. His name was Ronnie, and the appointment request didn't have many details except "I need help." I actually liked when the requests were vague because it gave me a challenge to look forward to.

Ronnie walked in for his appointment, and he looked just as I had imagined: a bit of a twink, shorter than I was but with extremely tan skin. He had a great smile, making him attractive for a little guy. I wasn't normally interested in twinks, but something about him got me going a bit. And to top everything else off, his southern accent made me melt. I introduced myself and led him into the therapy room.

We exchanged small talk, something I like to do with all of my new patients before diving in. Ronnie was originally from Atlanta and had just recently moved here after a bad break-up. He said that he saw my cards at one of the bars and decided to make an appointment to help him get over his ex. Assuring him that I could absolutely help him conquer his issues, I asked that he trust me and my treatment plans.

I assumed he already knew a little bit about my methods.

Before we jumped into his recent relationship, I asked him to tell me how he and his ex-boyfriend met.

I was single the entire year before we met. After my prior relationship, I promised myself that I would stay single for an entire twelve months and work on becoming a better person. Sometimes that was really hard to do, but I wasn't going to back down from my goal.

Even though I swore I would stay single, nowhere in that promise did I say I wasn't going to mess around with guys. I'm a dude, and I love fucking, so that wasn't part of my promise. Honestly, I wanted to fuck as many guys as I could, and in Atlanta, that actually wasn't very easy. Guys in Atlanta are a different breed, which is part of the reason I decided to move out here. They're very shallow, and they make a huge deal

I Think I'm a Serial Swiper

if you live outside of the "gay zone," as if driving 15 minutes for a hook-up is a big deal.

I guess I became a bit of a "serial swiper" as my friends would call it. I wasn't having any luck on the apps and thought that maybe I was just being too picky, so I started swiping right on every single guy. I honestly didn't care who the guy was— as long as he was clean, I wanted to fuck. But even with that, I still only fucked 30 guys during that 12-month period.

Thirty guys in a year? That was quite a bit. I hadn't even slept with that many people in my life—men and women combined. But I guess being in two long-term relationships put a bit of a damper on getting my numbers up. I'm not sure if I should have been happy or sad at the fact that his one-year "defeat" was more than my entire sexual life.

Before I slept with that first guy, I decided that I would take notes in my phone about each guy—physical description, dick details, and a rating to determine if he'd be a repeat.

As Ronnie was talking about his repeats, he took out his phone and handed it to me. On the screen, I saw the notepad with a long list of descriptions. The first one read, "Tall, short curved dick. Won't fuck again." Then another read, "Indian, smelled like curry but gave good head." The list went on and on—all 30 men, all with descriptions, and only a few that said he'd fuck them again.

"Is your ex-boyfriend on this list?" Ronnie nodded yes, gesturing for me to scroll to the last guy on the list. I looked back down at the phone and read the description: "Hispanic. Loves Mariah Carey. Fucked me ten ways. Maybe see again." If he was only a "maybe," then why date?

We matched on Tinder but formally met on Instagram. His name is Ramon. We're both huge Mariah Carey fans and followed each other for months before we started talking. He lived about four hours away from me, and it just seemed right to meet up since we both had similar interests.

"Tell me about the first time you had sex with him."

After talking for a few months, we decided to meet. He came to visit me in Atlanta, but I didn't let him come until the end of my one-year promise. We had really good conversations, and I developed feelings for him before we actually met, so I wanted to be at the end of my promise, just in case it led anywhere.

We didn't have sex right away. He stayed with me for the entire weekend since he lived so far away, and I just wanted to take it easy. Besides, I had just gotten my hole pounded the night before by my neighbor. We went to dinner, and he seemed like such a romantic guy. He held my hand on the drive back, and I was sure this was going to be some of the best sex I ever had.

When we got back to my place and went into the bedroom, he started kissing me. While he was on top of me kissing me, I kept trying to thrust my cock up into him, hoping that he would make his way down, but he didn't. I was super hard and really wanted him to suck me off. He just kept kissing me, and when he pulled my shorts down, I thought for sure that was it.

He moved down toward my throbbing dick, but just as he got to it, he grabbed my hips and flipped me over, spreading my ass cheeks and diving right into my hole with his tongue. Don't get me wrong—it felt amazing. But I really wanted him to suck on my dick. He ate my ass for about five minutes, and then slid up so his head was pressing against my hole. He spit down in his hand, rubbed it on his head, and then shoved his cock right into my hole. It kind of hurt, but at that point, I would take whatever I could get.

He pulled my hips back so I was on all fours and pounded my ass for about thirty seconds. He pulled his dick out and flipped me onto my back, and I thought for sure he was going to devour my cock. Wrong. He lifted my legs over his shoulders and then shoved his cock right back into my hole.

I grabbed my dick and started stroking it, and I actually thought I was going to cum pretty quickly. Just as I was getting close, he popped his cock out of my ass and told me to get on top.

I started riding him, and I swear he wanted to change positions every 60 seconds. It was exhausting. After going back and forth in different positions for literally a half hour, I finally told him he needed to hurry up or I was tapping out. He pushed me flat on my stomach, and after about two more minutes, shot his load up my hole and flooded my ass. At this point, I was so exhausted I didn't even care that I didn't get off.

The next morning, he asked if I enjoyed the sex, and I said yes because it actually wasn't horrible. I asked him if he'd blow me since I didn't get to cum the night before, and he gave me a disgusted look. He told me that he didn't suck dick, and I literally laughed at him until I realized he was serious. I asked why, but he wouldn't give me a straight answer beyond saying he was bi-sexual and just didn't like sucking dick. I had been with bi guys before, but most of them jumped at the chance of having a cock in their mouth. He then said that he was a total top, so he hoped that I was okay with that. I'm 95% bottom, so that was fine, although sometimes I just really wanted a nice ass to pound.

I'm still not sure why, but we ended up dating for over a year. In that entire year, he never sucked my dick, and he never let me fuck him, but for some reason, I still stayed with him. Things got pretty bad, and our relationship just sucked, so I finally broke up with him and decided to start fresh here in San Fran. I don't want another year of fucking and taking notes, Doc. I just want a normal relationship, and hopefully one that I get to top in.

This guy had obviously been through quite a bit in this relationship, and it was hard to believe that someone so cute could have been treated that way. Our time was up, but I told him we would continue our conversation and figure out how to assist him next time. He made an appointment for the following

I Think I'm a Serial Swiper

Friday, and as he left, I started planning out his treatment plan.

Chapter 5

RONNIE

The day before Ronnie's next appointment, he called to tell me he was having car trouble and wouldn't be able to make it into the office. I knew he needed my help and didn't want him to have to reschedule. I normally didn't do house calls, but I offered to have the appointment at his place. He quickly accepted, so I told him to send me his address, and I would be there at his scheduled time.

I asked Rocky if he wanted to go with me to the appointment, but he said he was actually going on a date that night. I was kind of shocked—I knew he had been fucking a lot of dudes, but didn't think he'd be ready to actually start dating and getting to know a guy on that level. I was really happy for him and told him I wanted to know every single detail. But literally as we were having the conversation, I heard his dating app go off, and soon he was flying out the door for another hookup. All I could do was shake my head, but I had definitely been there before.

The following morning, I headed over to Ronnie's apartment. He lived about a half hour north of me in a cute little complex surrounded by woods. I pulled up to his building and walked up to his third-floor unit. As I knocked on the door, I could hear him rustling around inside, and when the door opened, I saw two little cats rubbing on his legs. He shook my hand and invited me in, thanking me for coming over to his place for the appointment. He said he knew

I was able to help him and was happy he didn't have to reschedule.

Ronnie immediately began talking about Ramon, and I could tell how much anger he had built up inside from that relationship. He said he had gone on a few dates since Ramon, but they never led to anything. He told me that Ramon called him the night before and asked if he still loved him, then told Ronnie that he had been dating someone for the last couple months. I hated stuff like this. Honestly, this Ramon guy was just a complete piece of shit in my eyes.

I could hear the hurt and anger in Ronnie's voice as he spoke about Ramon. I suddenly decided to take a different route in my treatment plan. Standing up, I moved next to Ronnie on the couch and put my arm around him. He laid his head down on my shoulder, and I told him that I knew exactly how he felt. I informed him that the first step in being able to move past all this hurt was to release all of the frustrations he had from his relationship with Ramon.

I rolled myself off the couch and got down on my knees in front of him, pressing his body back into a more comfortable position on the couch. The look in his eyes showed total confusion. He had no clue what was about to happen. I rubbed my hands down his chest then on top of his cock, outlined through his gym shorts.

"Ramon never sucked your dick, right?" I asked him.

I leaned forward and started licking the outline of his cock through his shorts. I could feel his body tense up a bit, but then he moved his hand to the back of my head, forcing my head down on his tool. I pulled his shorts down to see that he wasn't wearing any underwear, exposing his already erect cock. I quickly engulfed his dick with my mouth, and his body instantly began to squirm. He never released the back of my head as he let out some of the loudest moans I have ever heard. This poor guy really just went an entire year without a blowjob.

I slobbered up and down on his shaft, teasing his head with my tongue and then going down towards his balls. I grabbed onto his cock and started stroking it as I was mouth deep with his balls, and then went back up and sucked on it some more. He was still squirming, and he pulled me up toward his face to make out with me. He shoved his tongue down my throat, and I straddled his lap for a good five minutes as we passionately kissed each other's lips and necks.

I got up for a second and pulled my pants and briefs off before sitting back down on his lap. He pushed my chest back a bit, grabbed onto my cock and started sucking it. I didn't waste any time, standing up so I could start fucking his face, grabbing the back of his head and forcing my tool straight down his throat.

I Think I'm a Serial Swiper

He didn't even let out a single gag, and God knows I wanted to shoot my load straight down his throat, but that wasn't part of my plan.

I let him suck on my cock for another few minutes, then stood and told him to go get some lube. I've never seen someone run so fast for something. He came back, laid down on the couch, and started lubing up his hole, but I shook my head, telling him no. I grabbed the lube from him and poured it all over his cock, stroking to rub it in and then putting some on my own hole. I knelt down on the couch with my head on the back cushion and ass in the air and told him it was time for him to top.

He jumped up, got behind me, and didn't waste any time. Before I knew it, his hard cock was deep in my hole, moving in and out—his hands on my hips with the occasional reach around to stroke my cock. He was pretty forceful, and with each thrust into my hole, I could tell that he was getting close to cumming—rightfully so after waiting a year to fuck someone.

He let out a loud moan and started pumping his cock faster and harder, and I could feel his warm load flooding my hole. He kept fucking me, and I could feel the cum starting to drip down my leg. He pulled his dick out, then laid down on the couch beside me, grabbing his legs to prop them in the air.

"Your turn."

I was already close to cumming, so I got down and shoved my cock into his warm hole and started pumping in and out. His dick was still hard, he started stroking it, and I was shocked to see that him shooting another load all over his chest. The sight of that really got me going, and out of nowhere, I started shooting my load deep into his hole, letting out a moan that was even louder than his.

I Think I'm a Serial Swiper

I leaned down and started kissing him, my hard cock still inside him. I pulled out and started licking up some of the cum from his chest, taking it up and making out with him with my cum-covered lips. This went on for another 30 minutes, and I honestly didn't want to leave, but I knew I had another appointment.

I hopped in the shower, and he came in behind me, pushing me against the wall and making out with me some more. Was this just a typical appointment, or would this turn into something more? I really didn't know what to think—I was always really good at separating this part of work from my personal life. But as I walked back to my car, I got a notification on my phone, and Ronnie had already scheduled another appointment for the following week with a note that read, "House call, please."

Chapter 6

JOHN

I rushed back to the office as fast as I could to make sure I wasn't late for my next appointment. Normally, I like to give myself extra time to prepare, but I was obviously preoccupied. When I walked up to the office, I saw a guy sitting on the bench next to the door and assumed he was my patient. As I got closer to the door, I realized that this was a repeat patient–John, Ryan's boyfriend. Ryan—the guy that Rocky was fucking in my office just a few days earlier.

I Think I'm a Serial Swiper

Now I felt pretty bad. I could tell John was feeling down by the way he sat, and I could only assume his relationship wasn't in the best place. What I had witnessed in my office technically wasn't the first time Rocky and Ryan had been together, seeing how they fucked each other during their last therapy session. And in that same session, John and I had flip-fucked each other, so my emotions were a little scattered too. I was also still thinking about how fantastic a lay Ronnie was.

I opened the office door and told John to come in. He didn't say anything, showing himself back to the room. I stopped by my desk to check something on my computer, grabbed my clipboard, and walked into the therapy room. John was already lying down on the couch with his arm up over his eyes. I sat down in my chair and asked him what was going on.

I'm pretty sure Ryan is cheating on me. After our last session, our sex life seemed to be doing pretty well. We were equally taking turns topping one another, and things seemed to be alright. I thought we were on the right track, but a few weeks later, it seemed like Ryan wanted to bottom ALL THE TIME. I always want to bottom too, but I knew that we had to be equal in order to make this relationship work.

Finally, I just refused to top him anymore. We were still fooling around and blowing each other, but we haven't had physical intercourse in a few weeks now. He wants to bottom, and I want to bottom, and I'm just tired of giving in and having to be the top. I know it sounds silly. In our last session, topping you felt really good, and I thought I could play the part more often. But I just can't. I need to bottom, too.

"Why do you think he's cheating on you?" I asked.

Out of nowhere, Ryan started going to the gym. A lot. And at weird times. Like sometimes he will wake up at 5am to go to the gym. Ryan's never been an early morning person, and when he was working out before, he would always go at night. Honestly, I'm just having a hard time trusting him, and over the past few weeks, he's stopped asking me to top him, which makes me think he's getting his fix somewhere else.

Well, of course he was getting his fix somewhere else. He was getting it right on the same sofa that John sat on, practically in the same spot. Shit, he might even be sitting in Ryan's cum stain because the cleaners hadn't been by since Rocky and Ryan were going at it.

I asked John how long it had been since he had bottomed. He said it had been over a month, and he was really craving a hard dick up his ass. I put my clipboard down on the table next to my chair, got up, and walked over in front of him. He already knew what to do. He sat up, took off my belt, and pulled my pants down, grabbing my dick and slowly stroking it. Thank God I had showered at Ronnie's because that could have been awkward.

He started licking the tip of my cock, teasing it and grabbing onto my balls, slightly pulling them, which felt really good. He slowly shoved my entire dick into his mouth, and I could feel it press against the back of his throat. He held it here for a second before slowly coming back up for some air. He sucked on my tool slowly, gradually picking up the pace, and I grabbed the back of his head to take some of the control away and started thrusting my hips back and forth, watching my cock go in and out of his mouth.

I could see him rubbing his own cock, so I knelt down in front of him and ripped off his shorts, exposing his beautiful, hard tool. I pushed him back into the couch and went to town on his dick, sucking the life out of it. I grabbed onto him and stroked it with the motion of my mouth while he held on tight to the back of my head.

I grabbed the backs of his legs and threw them up over my shoulders so I could get to his

I Think I'm a Serial Swiper

sweet hole. I put his balls in my mouth, sucking on them while I kept stroking his cock, then released them and licked my way across his taint and down to his hole. He had a perfect, hairless hole, and it was super tight from not getting fucked in a while.

I swirled my tongue around the outside of his hole, listening to him whimper as I got closer to the center. Making my way closer, I shoved my tongue in as far as I could. I wanted to get his ass so wet that we wouldn't even have to use lube. I licked that peach all over the place like it was my last meal, spitting on it and spitting in my hand to moisten my own cock.

I got up from his hole and kept his legs perched on top of my shoulders, spitting in my hand one last time to get my cock nice and wet. I told him he was going to fuck me, and we both laughed because we knew that obviously wasn't the point. I pressed my wet cock against his dripping hole and slowly inserted it. I was trying to be gentle since we weren't using lube, and I figured it would hurt him, but his moans were pure pleasure.

I pushed my dick deep into his hole until I couldn't get any further, then I paused there for a second, giving him a few extra moments to adjust. Apparently, he didn't need it because he began thrusting his hips and moving his hole back and forth on my piece. I should have figured because this was exactly what he had wanted. I grabbed him by his throat, gently, and let my hips move back and forth, thrusting my dick in and out of his hole. I'd pull my cock all the way out for a second, then shove it back in. His hole was so wet it felt like it was lubed up.

I fucked John for a few minutes and then wanted him to ride me. I pulled my dick out of his ass and sat down next to him on the couch, grabbing his arm and pulling him on top of me. He spit on his hand and rubbed my cock with it, getting it a little wetter, and then slowly lowered his hole down, devouring my rod. He started bouncing his ass up and down on my dick, and out of nowhere, the office door burst open. I grabbed John so he would stop moving and looked over my shoulder, only to see Rocky and Ryan standing at the door, both smiling.

Chapter 7

THE INTERRUPTION

We were like deer in headlights. Rocky and Ryan stood in the doorway, just looking at us. John turned around, my cock still fully inside of his hole, and said, "If you can't beat 'em, then join 'em." He turned back around so he was facing me and started riding my cock again. Was this all planned? Did he know Rocky and Ryan were fucking and just wanted to have an orgy again? Honestly, I really didn't care. I just needed to get another nut.

I Think I'm a Serial Swiper

Rocky and Ryan came into the room and shut the door behind them. Rocky sat down next to me on the couch, and John leaned over and started making out with him. Ryan got down on his knees behind John and started licking my dick and his hole, making his way down to my balls and then back up to where I was penetrating John.

Rocky started pulling off his pants, exposing that huge cock that was already hard while he was making out with John. He started stroking it, and before I knew it, John was getting off of my dick and moving over toward Rocky. He knelt down in front of Rocky and started devouring his cock, and Ryan didn't seem to care that I was just inside of his boyfriend—he was licking every inch of his boyfriend off my cock.

At one point, Rocky and I made this awkward eye contact with each other—which we both realized—then quickly made it a point not to look at one another. I was still sitting on the couch, and Ryan took his pants off and spun around so his legs were over the back of the couch and his ass was in my face—a bit of a couch-back 69 position. I dove right into his hole, which was stretched in a way that made me think that Rocky had already been inside of him today. He was still sucking on my dick as I was eating his peach, stroking my cock while he devoured it. John moved over and sucked on my balls while Rocky got up off the couch, got down behind John, and started eating his ass. That didn't last very long, and within seconds, Rocky reached for the lube and shoved his dick inside John's hole.

John never once dropped my balls out of his mouth, except to get a taste of my shaft. Rocky held on tight to his hips, thrusting himself in and out of John's hole. I smacked Ryan on the ass and told him it was time to go for a ride. He spun around and grabbed the lube from next to Rocky and poured it on my cock. At this point, I was exhausted, so I stayed on the couch and let Ryan climb aboard. He lowered his hole over my piece, and it was probably the loosest ass I had ever felt. He leaned over and whispered to me, "I want you to fuck me better than your brother can."

Challenge accepted.

I let Ryan ride my cock for a whole five seconds, then I grabbed onto him and stood up, never letting my cock fall out of his ass, and started bouncing him up and down. We fell back down onto the couch. I threw his legs over my shoulders and drilled him as fast and as hard as I could. Rocky was still fucking John from behind, which I'm assuming was one of his favorite positions because he spoke about it a lot. Ryan let out some of the loudest moans I had ever heard, and just as I said I was going to blow, Ryan pushed me out of his hole and pulled my cock up toward his face and started stroking it, completely covering his face with my load. I must have shot out a good six or seven squirts, and Ryan used his hands to push it down into his mouth. He leaned forward and started sucking on my cock, completely draining every last drop out of it.

Looking over, I could tell Rocky was about to cum from the look on his face. He let out a few loud moans, and then made one final thrust into John's ass. I'm not sure if John got to blow his load, and at that point, I really didn't care. I realized I didn't even give Ryan a chance to cum. The way I saw it, I was tapping out, and they could go home and take care of each other. Either that, or they could always invite Rocky back to their place.

Chapter 8

DREW

As I walked back into my building that night after a long and exhausting day, a car pulled up along the sidewalk where I was. I wasn't sure if it was random, or someone following me, and then I recognized the driver.

It was Sean. The guy with herpes.

He rolled down his window and said hi, and we made a little small talk. He asked me if I wanted to come over to his house and offered to drive me back home the next morning. Not only was I exhausted and all sexed out, but I really didn't want anything to do with his ass. He wasn't taking no for an answer and said things like he missed me and really wanted to spend time with me. This bitch didn't even know me! I finally just told him I wasn't interested, and that I also didn't appreciate him waiting to tell me that he had herpes after blowing a load in my ass. I walked into the building, and he drove away.

After I showered and cleaned all the sex off of me (and out of me), I grabbed my phone and opened up the dating app. I honestly thought about deleting it for a while and just taking a break. After all, I was getting more action from my patients than I was from the app.

I must have swiped for a good thirty minutes, surprisingly swiping left, because nothing was really sparking any joy. I was about to put my phone on the nightstand and go to bed when this one profile popped up and caught my eye.

I Think I'm a Serial Swiper

Drew.

He was tall. His profile said 6'3". He had super tan skin, a gorgeous smile, and possible Italian ancestry. Probably an Italian stallion for that matter. His profile was funny, his photos were cute, and he just looked like an all-around wholesome guy. I swiped right, and no sooner did I put my phone down to go to sleep did he message me. Damn, he must have been thinking the same things about me that I was thinking about him.

I grabbed my phone, opened the app back up, and saw a message that read, "You're adorable." I am adorable, and he was too. We stayed up and chatted back and forth for almost three hours, and for the first time in a long time, I felt something more than just wanting a hook-up. I felt like this was something that could be real.

Drew lived about two hours away from me, and we talked all day, non-stop, for the entire next week. We made plans that I would go visit him for the weekend, and it was nearly inevitable that he was going to be my boyfriend. Around the fifth day of talking to each other, we exchanged dick pics, and I was definitely right in thinking he was Italian–his sausage practically hung down to his knees. Or, as he would joke around, "it's like a baby's arm holding an apple." Regardless, I knew I was going to thoroughly enjoy playing with that horse cock.

The following weekend rolled around, and I drove over to see him. We joked around that we weren't going to have sex the first time we met because we both agreed that this was going to be way different. We even joked that we could shower together, but we would have to wear bathing suits.

I pulled down the road that Drew lived on and parked my car in guest parking. As I got out of the car, I saw him walking from his townhouse, just as cute as could be. He walked up to me and gave me a big hug and kiss. He grabbed my bag for me, and we walked inside.

He introduced me to his roommate Brittany. I was a little nervous because I didn't know she was going to be there. But she was only grabbing a few things and said she was going to stay with her boyfriend for the weekend. I assume this was planned. She was really sweet, and I could see why they were such good friends.

We went out to dinner, then came back and just listened to music and drank wine. I leaned over and just started kissing him, and he pulled me over so that I was straddling him and stuck his tongue down my throat. We had one of the most passionate make out sessions I've experienced. I could feel his dick getting hard against mine, and I started slowly moving my hips back and forth, rubbing them together.

I got up, grabbed his hand, and led him into his bedroom. He laid me down on the bed and then got on top of me and started kissing me again. It was purely romantic. I pulled off his shirt, and he kicked off his pants. He got up, pulled all of my clothes off, and leaned back down to start kissing me again. The feeling of our naked bodies rubbing against one another was almost euphoric.

We must have made out for a good 15 or 20 minutes. He started kissing on my neck and kissed his way down my chest to my cock. When he got down there, he grabbed the base, looked up at me, and said, "Now that's a triumphant bastard." We both just laughed, and he slowly swallowed my dick into his mouth until his lips were touching my base. He went up and down on my dick, and I really wanted to suck on his– it was even bigger when it was hard.

After a few minutes of him swallowing my cock, I pushed him over on his back and dove straight down for his dick. I couldn't even get half of it in my mouth because of its monster size, but fuck if he didn't moan and grunt each time my mouth went up and down. I was certainly ready for the challenge and wanted that Italian monster inside of me, pronto.

I looked up at him, taking a break from sucking his dick to tell him I wanted him to fuck me. He gave me an odd look, almost a frown. I asked him what was wrong, and he told me that he was a bottom and didn't like topping. How did I not know this? How is this not something that we had discussed? I mean, it wasn't a deal breaker for me—I'm a firm believer that when it comes to sex positions, gay men should do whatever feels right. I considered myself a super versatile guy who just went with the flow. But, he was just a bottom? Like, if we dated, I was never going to get my hole filled?

Obviously, I didn't let him know what I was thinking, saying instead, "That's okay. I want to feel that hole anyway." I flipped him over and dove down between his ass cheeks, spreading them far so I could get a nice glimpse of his perfectly smooth hole. I shoved my tongue right in it, and his back arched, tossing his ass into my face a little bit. I licked his hole up and down, tongue fucking it until it was nice and wet and ready to be fucked.

I didn't bring any condoms with me, since I figured he'd be the one topping, especially with his horse cock. I knew he wasn't going to want to bareback the first time, so I asked him for a condom. He reached into his drawer, and I could see the gold wrapper as he tossed it over toward me.

A magnum.

Now, my dick was pretty decent, but not decent enough to fill up a magnum. I asked him if he had anything else, and he just smiled at me. Whatever. I ripped it open, slid it down my shaft, and to my surprise, it actually fit alright. Drew grabbed the lube and stroked my cock a bit, then he pulled his own legs back, so I could get into his hole. It didn't take much effort, and my slimy dick slipped right in. Drew let out a huge sigh of relief. He was really tight, which made the condom fit my cock a little better.

Wrapping my arms around his legs to prop them up, I started thrusting my dick in and out of his hole, leaning down and passionately kissing him while I fucked him. Actually, we made love—I thought that was what making love felt like. As we kept going at it, I could feel the condom getting a little loose. I pulled out of his ass to adjust the condom, and then said, "Fuck it." I ripped the condom off and tossed it on the floor. His ass was full of lube, so I didn't need to put any on my bare dick. I rolled over on my back and told him to sit on it.

Drew got up off his back, threw his leg over me, and slid down my shaft with ease. I hadn't worn a condom in quite a long time, and fuck if his ass didn't feel amazing immediately after tearing that shit off. His cock was fully hard, and he stroked it as he bounced up and down on my member.

I knew it wasn't going to take him long, and within a few minutes, he was screaming and shooting his load all over the place, covering me from my nose down to where his dick bounced off my stomach. Naturally, I had my mouth open, and his cum tasted pretty good—I knew I had seen some pineapple juice in his fridge.

I was close but not quite ready yet, so I flipped him over onto his back and started going pretty hard on his hole. Within a minute, I reached my climax, let out a loud scream, and shot my load right up his hole. He immediately asked if I had cum inside of him, and I laughed a little and said yes. "I didn't know you were going to cum inside of me—I wish you would have pulled out." I just shrugged my shoulders. After all, I was pretty sure this guy was going to be my boyfriend, and if I was going to be the top, I'd be shooting my load wherever I damn well pleased.

I Think I'm a Serial Swiper

We spent the rest of the weekend together and must have had sex seven more times before I headed back to the city on Sunday, each time shooting my load right into his raw hole. He definitely wasn't complaining about it, and I hoped he'd finally get in the mood to top, but I wasn't going to hold my breath.

I came back to see him the following weekend because he wanted to introduce me to some of his friends. I was excited to meet them, but when we got to the restaurant, I saw three girls sitting at the table with the biggest, cuntiest looks I had ever seen.

"Hunter, meet Hope, Dina, and Katlyn."

I could already tell this wasn't going to end well.

Author Bio

Grayson Ace has had his fair share of sexcapades, and figured why not write about them? Recently divorced, he is re-discovering himself (and plenty of hot men) and creating many new sexy adventures along the way. If you like what you see, please leave a review, and you never know....you may end up in one of the stories!

GraysonAce.com
Facebook: Grayson Ace
Instagram: graysonaceofficial
Twitter: @GraysonAce1

MORE BOOKS FROM GRAYSON ACE

How I Got Here

First Year Out of the Closet

You're Only a Top?

You're Only a Bottom?

I Think I'm a Serial Swiper

Lookin' in All the Wrong Places

What Makes Me a Whore?

A Breach in Confidentiality

Back Door Pass

My European Adventure

An Unexpected Affair

More to come!

4 HORSEMEN PUBLICATIONS

LGBT EROTICA

LEO SPARX

Claiming Alexander
Taming Alexander
Saving Alexander

EROTICA

ALI WHIPPE

Office Hours
Tutoring Center
Athletics
Extra Credit
Bound for Release
Fetish Circuit

Dalia Lance

My Home on Whore Island
Slumming It on Slut Street
Training of the Tramp
The Imperfect Perfection
72% Match
It Was Meant To Be... Or Whatever

Chastity Veldt

Molly in Milwaukee
Irene in Indianapolis
Lydia in Louisville
Natasha in Nashville

Honey Cummings

Sleeping with Sasquatch
Cuddling with Chupacabra
Naked with New Jersey Devil
Laying with the Lady in Blue
Wanton Woman in White
Beating it with Bloody Mary
Beau and Professor Bestialora
The Goat's Gruff
Goldie and Her Three Beards
Pied Piper's Pipe
Princess Pea's Bed
Jack's Beanstalk

4HorsemenPublications.com

www.ingramcontent.com/pod-product-compliance
Lightning Source LLC
LaVergne TN
LVHW041542060526
838200LV00037B/1098